anythink

For Mom and Dad. Thank you for showing me the world is
full of endless opportunities.

-KC

For Tim P. — master of the slopes

-JLE

MacLaren-Cochrane Publishing

Text © 2017 Kim Constantinesco

Cover and Interior Art © 2017 Jessica Linn Evans

Solar the Polar

MacLaren-Cochrane Publishing
620 Buchanan Way, Folsom, CA 95630

Library of Congress Control Number: 2017951937

First Edition

ISBN
Hardcover: 978-1-365-86182-6
Softcover: 978-1-365-86184-0

For orders, visit
www.maclaren-cochranepublishing.com
www.facebook.com/maclaren-cochranepublishing

Solar the Polar

By Kim Constantinesco

Illustrated by
Jessica Linn Evans

Solar the Polar was an Arctic bear,

Born way up north in the land of cold air.

As a Polar snowboarder, his life there was lonely,

In his favorite sport, he was the one-and only!

When Solar's half-pipe melted into sea foam,
He knew he must leave to look for a new home.

Where would he be safe? Where could he go?
He needed a high spot in mountains of snow.

So he headed south, roaming
for weeks, to a shimmering range of
glaciers and peaks.

Solar loved this new place, but he wanted a friend
To share his snowboarding from morning to end.

Each day he'd head out to shred down the hill,
Carving turns on steep slopes was always a thrill.

Finally one sunny day, Solar spotted a girl twirling a sit-ski down-slope with a swirl. Then Solar looked twice...did he really see? She was missing a leg below each of her knees!

He followed her tracks, not crowding her space,
just hoping to catch up and meet face to face.

"I'm Solar," he said, when he got the chance, "and I like what I saw of your style at first glance"

"Please don't be scared of me…I'm a cool bear, I moved down from the north…it's too warm up there."

"Hi. My name is Sunny," she said, with a smile, "maybe we both can chill out for a while."

"My sit-ski takes me wherever I go from the top of the peaks to this valley below!"

Solar grabbed up his gear.

"Let's go for a ride! Now you have a Polar Bear guide at your side!"

Sunny's legs didn't work perfectly right, but on her sit-ski,
what a magical sight!
So Solar became Sunny's backcountry buddy, and he
pushed her along when the snow got too cruddy!

Schussing through powder and tall evergreens, the
pair motored down like lean mean machines.

One day in a storm, they heard a loud rumble, the snow wall above them collapsed in a tumble.

"AVALANCHE!" Sunny yelled, spinning away fast, If they didn't race, this run would be their last.

Solar pushed off a mogul and flew on his board, just at the last moment he jumped, and he soared.

Safe! Solar landed away from the slide, but he couldn't see Sunny... She was not by his side.

Snow waves came to a stop. All was perfectly still.
No movement in sight anywhere on the hill.

Solar's polar heart pounded...
Where was his friend? He had to act fast or it was the end. This girl was
special, so totally brave, not afraid to be different, a soul he must save.

He sniffed through the drifts to find any trace, caught a whiff of her scent in just the right place.

With his giant paws, he dug deep through the rubble, giving his all to get her out of trouble.

The tip of one sit-ski poked out, then two, Sunny's helmet and goggles came into view. Solar pulled her out gently, she would be fine, the mighty bear rescued the girl just in time.

From that moment on, the friends never forgot that is why backcountry safety is taught.
They both understood that there's a good reason to ski with a buddy in high winter season.

Solar hugged Sunny.

"I'm glad you're okay. Let's hang it up for the rest of the day."

Sunny hugged Solar.

"I want to give back, so if it's up to me,
Tomorrow I'll teach you to ride a sit-ski!

THE END

Kim Constantinesco
Author

Kim Constantinesco did the bulk of her childhood reading with bed covers over her head and a flashlight in hand. Curious George and the Man with the Yellow Hat occupied her cocoon and helped foster her deep love for unabated adventure and exploration. Kim is the editor-in-chief of a digital publication that tells the inspiring stories in sports. She enjoys putting the spotlight on the athletes, coaches, and fans who overcome the odds and make a positive difference in the world. She is a big mountain snowboarder who had a near tragic accident on the slopes only to return to the mountain and compete at a high level. She grew up in Salt Lake City and has a masters degree in health psychology from Northern Arizona University. She now lives in Denver, and can be found doing backflips on her snowboard in the winter and hiking 14,000-foot mountains in the summer.

Jessica Linn Evans
Illustrator

Jessica Linn Evans was born and raised in the Pacific Northwest of the United States where she grew up into a love of the outdoors and fairy stories, a penchant for illustration, and an eye for detail. She graduated from the University of Idaho with a BFA in Studio Arts. After many years in the role of Art Director/Graphic Designer, she moved forward full-time with her passion for illustrating and writing books for children, creating whimsical characters and settings, emphasizing the wonder of the natural world. Jessica resides in Idaho with her husband Ed and four delightful children.

See more of Jessica's art at https://jessicalinnevans.com/

CPSIA information can be obtained
at www.ICGtesting.com
Printed in the USA
LVHW07n2312040718
582674LV00012B/312/P